Previously published as *Horrid Henry's Head Lice*

Francesca Simon

Illustrated by Tony Ross

SCHOLASTIC INC.

New York Toronto London Auckland Sydney
Mexico City New Delhi Hong Kong

"Horrid Henry's Secret Club" was first published in
Horrid Henry's Secret Club in Great Britain by Orion Children's Books in 1996.
"Horrid Henry's Head Lice" and "Horrid Henry's School Trip" were first published
in *Horrid Henry's Nits* in Great Britain by Orion Children's Books in 1997.
"Mood Margaret Moves In" was first published in *Horrid Henry and the Tooth Fairy*
in Great Britain by Orion Children's Books in 1997.

ISBN 0-439-22416-0

Published by Scholastic Inc., 555 Broadway, New York, NY 10012,
by arrangement with Hyperion Books for Children,
an imprint of Disney Children's Book Group, LLC.

12 11 10 9 8 7 6 5 4 3 2 1 1 2 3 4 5 6/0

Printed in the U.S.A. 40

First Scholastic printing, September 2001

Also by Francesca Simon:

Horrid Henry

Horrid Henry Strikes It Rich

CONTENTS

Chapter 1

HORRID HENRY AND THE SECRET CLUB

"Halt! Who goes there?"

"Me."

"Who's me?" asked Moody Margaret.

"ME!" said Sour Susan.

"What's the password?"

"Uhhhh . . ." Sour Susan paused. What was the password? She thought and thought and thought.

"Potatoes?"

Margaret sighed loudly. **Why was she friends with such a stupid person?**

"No it isn't."

"Yes it is," said Susan.

"'Potatoes' was last week's password," said Margaret.

"No it wasn't."

"Yes it was," said Moody Margaret. "It's my club and I decide."

There was a long pause.

"All right," said Susan sourly. "What *is* the password?"

"I don't know if I'm going to tell you," said Margaret. "I could be giving away a big secret to the enemy."

"But I'm not the enemy," said Susan. "I'm Susan."

"*Shhhh!*" said Margaret. "We don't want Henry to find out who's in the secret club."

Susan looked quickly over her shoulder. The enemy was nowhere to be seen. She whistled twice.

"All clear," said Sour Susan. "Now let me in."

Moody Margaret thought for a moment. Letting someone in without the password broke the first club rule.

"Prove to me you're Susan, and not the enemy pretending to be Susan," said Margaret.

"You *know* it's me!" wailed Susan.

"Prove it."

Susan stuck her foot into the tent.

"I'm wearing the black patent-leather shoes with the blue flowers I always wear."

"No good," said Margaret. "The enemy could have stolen them."

"I'm speaking with Susan's voice and I look like Susan," said Susan.

"No good," said Margaret. "The enemy could be a master of disguise."

Susan stamped her foot. "And I know that you were the one who pinched Helen and I'm going to tell Miss . . ."

"Come closer to the tent flap," said Margaret.

Susan bent over.

"Now listen to me," said Margaret. "Because I'm only going to tell you once. **When a secret club member wants to come in, they say, 'Nunga.'** Anyone inside answers back, 'Nunga Nu.' That's how I know it's you and you know it's me."

"Nunga," said Sour Susan.

"Nunga Nu," said Moody Margaret. "Enter."

Susan entered the club. She gave the secret handshake, sat down on her box, and sulked.

"You knew it was me all along," said Susan.

Margaret scowled at her.

"That's not the point. If you don't want to obey the club rules, you can leave."

Susan didn't move.

"Can I have a cookie?" she said.

Margaret smiled graciously. "Have two," she said. "Then we'll get down to business."

Meanwhile, hidden under a bush behind some strategically placed branches, another top-secret meeting was taking place in the yard next door.

"I think that's everything," said the leader. "I shall now put the plans into action."

"What am I going to do?" said Perfect Peter.

"Stand guard," said Horrid Henry.

"I always have to stand guard," said Peter as the leader crept out. "It's not fair."

"Have you brought your spy report?" asked Margaret.

"Yes," said Susan.

"Read it aloud," said Margaret.

Susan took out a piece of paper and read: "I watched the enemy's house for two hours yesterday morning."

"Which morning?" interrupted Margaret.

"Saturday morning," said Susan. "A lady with gray hair and a beret walked past."

"What color was the beret?" said Margaret.

"I don't know," said Susan.

"You call yourself a spy and you don't know what color the beret was?" said Margaret.

"Can I please continue with my report?" said Susan.

"I'm not stopping you," said Margaret.

"Then I saw the enemy leave the house with his brother and mother. The enemy kicked his brother twice. His mother shouted at him. Then I saw the mailman—"

"NUNGA!" screeched a voice from outside.

Margaret and Susan froze.

"NUNGA!!!" screeched the voice again. "I know you're in there!"

"Aaaahh!" squeaked Susan. "It's Henry!"

"Quick! Hide!" hissed Margaret.

The secret spies crouched behind two boxes.

"You told him our password!" hissed Margaret. "How dare you!"

"Wasn't me!" hissed Susan. "I couldn't even remember it, so how could I have told him? You told him!"

"Didn't," hissed Margaret.

"NUNGA!!!" screeched Henry again. "You have to let me in! I know the password."

"What do we do?" hissed Susan. "You said anyone who knows the password enters."

"For the last time, NUN-GAAAAA!" shouted Horrid Henry.

"Nunga Nu," said Margaret. "Enter."

Henry swaggered into the tent. Margaret glared at him.

"Don't mind if I do," said Henry, grabbing all the chocolate cookies and stuffing them into his

mouth. Then he sprawled on the rug, scattering crumbs everywhere.

"What are you doing?" said Horrid Henry.

"Nothing," said Moody Margaret.

"Nothing," said Sour Susan.

"You are, too," said Henry.

"Mind your own business," said Margaret. "Now, Susan, let's vote on whether to allow boys in. I vote no."

"I vote no, too," said Susan.

"Sorry, Henry, you can't join. Now leave."

"No," said Henry.

"**Leave,**" said Margaret.

"Make me," said Henry.

Margaret took a deep breath. Then she opened her mouth and screamed. No one could scream as loud, or as long, or as piercingly, as Moody Margaret. After a few moments, Susan started screaming, too.

Henry got to his feet, knocking over the crate they used as a table.

"Watch out," said Henry. "Because the Black Hand will be back!" He turned to go.

Moody Margaret sprang up behind him and pushed him through the flap. Henry landed in a heap outside.

"Can't get me!" shouted Henry. He picked himself up and jumped over the wall. "The Black Hand is the best!"

"Oh yeah?" muttered Margaret. "We'll see about that."

Henry checked over his shoulder to make sure no one was watching. Then he crept back to his fort.

"**Smelly toads,**" he whispered to the guard.

The branches parted. Henry climbed in.

"Did you attack them?" said Peter.

"Of course," said Henry. "Didn't you hear Margaret screaming?"

"I was the one who heard their password, so I think I should have gone," said Peter.

"Whose club is this?" said Henry.

The corners of Peter's mouth began to turn down.

"So, get out!" said Henry.

"Sorry!" said Peter. "Please, Henry, can I be a real member of the Black Hand?"

"No," said Henry. "You're too young. And don't you dare come into the fort when I'm not here."

"I won't," said Peter.

"Good," said Henry. "Now, here's the plan. I'm going to set a booby trap in Margaret's tent. Then when she goes in . . ." Henry shrieked with laughter as he pictured Moody Margaret covered in cold muddy water.

All was not well back at Moody Margaret's secret club.

"It's your fault," said Margaret.

"It isn't," said Susan.

"You're such a blabbermouth, and you're a terrible spy."

"I am not," said Susan.

"Well, I'm leader, and I ban you from the club for a week for breaking our sacred rule and telling the enemy our password. Now go away."

"Oh please, let me stay," said Susan.

"No," said Margaret.

Susan knew there was no point arguing with Margaret when she got that horrible bossy look on her face.

"You're so mean," said Susan.

Moody Margaret picked up a book and started to read.

Sour Susan got up and left.

I know what I'll do to fix Henry, thought Margaret. I'll set a booby trap in Henry's fort. Then when he goes in . . . Margaret shrieked with laughter as she pictured Horrid Henry covered in cold muddy water.

Just before lunch Henry sneaked into Margaret's yard holding a plastic bucket of water and some string. He stretched the string just above the ground across the entrance and suspended the bucket above, with the other end of the string tied around it.

Just after lunch Margaret sneaked into Henry's yard holding a bucket of water and some string. She stretched the string across the fort's entrance

and rigged up the bucket. What she wouldn't give to see Henry soaking wet when he tripped over the string and pulled the bucket of water down on him.

Perfect Peter came into the yard carrying a ball. Henry wouldn't play with him and there was nothing to do.

Why shouldn't I go into the fort? thought Peter. I helped build it.

Next door, Sour Susan slipped into the yard. She was feeling sulky.

Why shouldn't I go into the tent? thought Susan. It's my club, too.

Perfect Peter walked into the fort and tripped.

CRASH! SPLASH!

Sour Susan walked into the tent and tripped.

CRASH! SPLASH!

Horrid Henry heard howls. He ran into the yard whooping.

"Ha! Ha! Margaret! Gotcha!"

Then he stopped.

Moody Margaret heard screams. She ran into the yard cheering.

"Ha! Ha! Henry! Gotcha!"

Then she stopped.

"That's it!" shrieked Peter. "I'm leaving!"

"But it wasn't me," said Henry.

"That's it!" sobbed Susan. "I quit!"

"But it wasn't me," said Margaret.
"Rats!" said Henry.
"Rats!" said Margaret.
They glared at each other.

Chapter 2

HORRID HENRY'S SCHOOL TRIP

"Don't forget my packed lunch for the school trip," shouted Horrid Henry for the tenth time. "I want chips, cookies, chocolate, and a fizzy drink."

"No way, Henry," said Dad grimly, slicing carrots. "I'm making you a healthy, nutritious lunch."

"But I don't want a healthy lunch," howled Henry. "I like sweets!"

"Sweets, yuck," said Perfect Peter. He peeked in his lunch box.

"Oh boy, an apple!" said Peter. "And egg salad on whole wheat bread with the crusts on! And carrot and celery sticks, my favorite! Thank you so much, Dad. Henry, if you don't eat healthy food, you'll never grow big and strong."

"Oh yeah?" said Henry. "I'll show you how big and strong I am, you little pip-squeak," he added, springing at Peter. He was a boa constrictor throttling his prey.

"Uggghhhh," choked Peter.

"Stop being horrid, Henry!" shouted Mom. "Or there will be no school trip for you."

Henry let Peter go. Horrid Henry loved school trips. No work. No assembly. A packed lunch. A chance to fool around all day. What could be better?

"I'm going to the Frosty Freeze Ice Cream factory," said Henry. "Free ice cream for everyone. Yippee!"

Perfect Peter made a face. "I don't like ice cream," he said. "My class is going somewhere much better—Our Town Museum. And Mom's coming to help."

"I'd rather be boiled alive and eaten by cannibals than go to that boring old dump," said Horrid Henry, shuddering. Mom had dragged him there once. Never again.

Then Henry noticed Peter's T-shirt. It was exactly the same as his, purple-striped with gold stars.

"Tell Peter to stop copying what I wear to school!" screamed Henry.

"It doesn't matter, Henry," said Mom. "You're going on different trips. No one will notice."

"Just keep out of my way, Peter," snarled Henry. "I don't want anyone to think we're related."

Horrid Henry's class buzzed with excitement as they scrambled to be first on the bus.

"I've got chips!" shouted Dizzy Dave.

"I've got cookies!" shouted Anxious Andrew.

"I've got toffee and chocolate and lollipops and three sodas!" shouted Greedy Graham.

"*WAAAA,*" wailed Weepy William. "I forgot my packed lunch."

"Quiet!" ordered Miss Battle-Axe as the bus started moving. "Sit still and behave. No eating on the bus. William, stop weeping."

"I need to go to the bathroom!" shouted Lazy Linda.

"Well, you'll have to wait," snapped Miss Battle-Axe.

Horrid Henry had trampled his way to the window seats at the back next to Rude Ralph and Greedy Graham. He liked those seats best. Miss Battle-Axe couldn't see him, and he could make faces at all the people in the cars behind him.

Henry and Ralph rolled down the window and chanted, **"Beans, beans, good for the heart, the more you eat, the more you—"**

"HENRY!" bellowed Miss Battle-Axe. "Turn around and face forward NOW!"

"I need to go to the bathroom!" shouted Dizzy Dave.

"Look what I've got, Henry," said Greedy Graham, holding a bulging bag of candy.

"Gimme some," said Henry.

"And me," said Rude Ralph.

The three boys stuffed their faces with candy.

"Ugh, a green lime," said Henry, taking the sticky candy out of his mouth. "Eeech." He flicked the candy away.

PING!

The candy landed on Moody Margaret's neck.

"Ow," said Margaret.

She turned around and glared at Henry.

"Stop it, Henry!" she snarled.

"I didn't do anything," said Henry.

PING!

A candy landed in Sour Susan's hair.

PING!

A candy stuck on Anxious Andrew's new sweater.

"Henry's throwing candy!" shouted Margaret.

Miss Battle-Axe turned around.

"Henry! Sit next to me," she said.

"I needed to go to the bathroom!" wailed Weepy William.

Finally, the bus drove up to the Frosty Freeze Factory. A gigantic, delicious-looking ice cream cone loomed above it.

"We're here!" shouted Henry.

"You scream! I scream! We all scream for ice cream!" shrieked the children as the bus stopped outside the gate.

"Why are we waiting here?" yelled Greedy Graham. "I want my ice cream now!"

Henry stuck his head out of the window. The gates were chained shut. A large sign read: CLOSED ON MONDAYS.

Miss Battle-Axe looked pale. "I don't believe this," she muttered.

"Class, there's been a mix-up, and we seem to have come on the wrong day," said Miss Battle-Axe. "But never mind. We'll go to—"

"The science museum!" shouted Clever Clare.

"The zoo!" shouted Dizzy Dave.

"Laser Zap!" shouted Horrid Henry.

"No," said Miss Battle-Axe. "Our Town Museum."

"Ugggghhhhh," groaned the class.

No one groaned louder than Horrid Henry.

The children left their jackets and lunch boxes in the lunchroom and then followed the museum guide to Room 1.

"First we'll see Mr. Jones's collection of rubber bands," said the guide. **"Then our famous display of door hinges and dog collars through history**. And don't worry, you'll be seeing our latest acquisitions, soil from Miss Montague's garden and the mayor's baby pictures."

Horrid Henry had to escape.

"I need to go to the bathroom," said Henry.

"Hurry up, then," said Miss Battle-Axe. "And come straight back. "

The toilets were next to the lunchroom.

Henry thought he'd make sure his lunch was still there. Yup, there it was, right next to Ralph's.

I wonder what Ralph has got, thought Henry, staring at Ralph's packed lunch. No harm in looking.

WOW. Rude Ralph's lunch box was bursting with chips, candy, and a chocolate-spread sandwich on white bread.

He'll feel sick if he eats all that junk food, thought Henry. I'd better help him.

It only took a second to swap Ralph's sandwich for Henry's egg salad.

This certainly isn't very healthy, thought Henry, gazing at Greedy Graham's goodies. I'll do him a favor and exchange a few of my celery sticks for his candy.

Just look at all those treats, thought Henry, lifting Sour Susan's cakes. She should eat a more balanced meal.

A pack of raisins zipped from Henry's lunch box to Susan's and a sticky bun leaped from Susan's to Henry's.

Tsk tsk, thought Henry, helping himself to Tough Toby's chocolate bar and replacing it with an apple. Too many sweets are bad for the teeth.

That's better, he thought, gazing at his repacked lunch with satisfaction. Then he strolled back to his class, who were gathered around a glass case.

"This is the soil in which Miss Montague grew

her prize-winning vegetables," droned the guide. "She grew squash, tomatoes, potatoes, leeks—"

"When do we eat?" interrupted Horrid Henry.

"I'm starving," whined Greedy Graham.

"My stomach's growling," groaned Rude Ralph.

"When's lunch?" moaned Moody Margaret.

"WE'RE HUNGRY!" wailed the children.

"All right," said Miss Battle-Axe. "We'll eat now."

The class stampeded down the hall and grabbed their lunches. Henry sat in a corner and tucked in.

For a moment there was silence, then the room echoed with howls of dismay.

"Where's my sticky bun?" yelped Sour Susan.

"My candy is gone!" screamed Greedy Graham.

"What's this? Egg salad? Yuck!" shouted Rude Ralph, hurling the sandwich at Anxious Andrew.

That did it. The room filled with flying carrot and celery sticks, granola bars, raisins, crusts,

and apples. Henry smirked as he wiped the last traces of chocolate from his mouth.

"Stop it! Stop it!" howled Miss Battle-Axe. "Well done, Henry, for being the only sensible child. You may lead us back to see the pieces of Roman pottery in Room 2."

Horrid Henry walked proudly at the head of the shuffling, whining children. Then he noticed the elevator at the far end. A sign read

STAFF ONLY: DO NOT ENTER

I wonder where that elevator goes, thought Horrid Henry.

"Stop him!" yelled a guard.

But it was too late.

Henry had dashed to the elevator and pressed the top button.

Up, up, up he zipped.

Henry found himself in a small room filled with half-finished exhibits. On display were lists of overdue library books, "lightbulbs from 1965 to today," and rows and rows of rocks.

Then, in the corner, Henry actually saw something interesting: a dog's skeleton protected by a drooping blue cord.

Henry looked more closely.

It's just a pile of bones, thought Henry.

He wobbled the blue cord, then stood on it.

"Look at me, I'm a tightrope walker," chortled Horrid Henry, swaying on the blue cord. "I'm the best tightrope walker in—*AGGGHHHH!*"

Horrid Henry lost his balance and toppled against the skeleton.

CLITTER-CLATTER! The bones crashed to the ground.

DING DING DING. A burglar alarm began to wail.

Museum guards ran into the room.

Uh-oh, thought Horrid Henry. He slipped between a guard's legs and ran. Behind him he could hear pounding feet.

Henry dashed into a large room filled with road signs, used bus tickets, and traffic cones. At the other end of the room Henry saw Peter's class gathered in front of "The Story of the Drain." Oh no. There was Mom.

Henry ducked behind the traffic cones.

Museum guards entered.

"There he is!" shouted one. "The boy in the purple T-shirt with the gold stars."

Henry stood fixed to the spot. He was trapped. Then the guards ran straight past his hiding place. A long arm reached over and plucked Perfect Peter from his group.

"Come with us, you!" snarled the guard. "We're going straight to the Bad Children's Room."

"But . . . but . . ." gasped Peter.

"No ifs or buts!" snapped the guard. "Who's in charge of this child?"

"I am," said Mom. "What's the meaning of this?"

"You come, too," ordered the guard.

"But . . . but . . ." gasped Mom.

Shouting and protesting, Mom and Perfect Peter were taken away.

Then Henry heard a familiar booming voice.

"Margaret, that's enough pushing," said Miss Battle-Axe. "No touching, Ralph. Stop weeping, William. Hurry up, everyone! The bus leaves in five minutes. Walk quietly to the exit."

Everyone immediately started running.

Horrid Henry waited until most of the children had charged past, then rejoined the group.

"Where have you been, Henry?" snapped Miss Battle-Axe.

"Just enjoying this great museum," said Horrid Henry. "When can we come back?"

Chapter 3

MOODY MARGARET MOVES IN

Mom was on the phone.

"Of course we'd be delighted to have Margaret," she said. "It will be no trouble at all."

Horrid Henry stopped breaking the tails off Perfect Peter's plastic horses.

"WHAT?" he howled.

"Shh, Henry," said Mom. "No, no," she added. "Henry is delighted, too. See you Friday."

"What's going on?" said Henry.

"Margaret is coming to stay while her parents go on vacation," said Mom.

Henry was speechless with horror.

"She's going to stay . . . here?"

"Yes," said Mom.

"How long?" said Henry.

"Two weeks," said Mom brightly.

Horrid Henry could not stand Moody Margaret for more than two minutes.

"Two weeks?" he said. **"I'll run away! I'll lock her out of the house, I'll pull her hair out, I'll . . ."**

"Don't be horrid, Henry," said Mom. "Margaret's a lovely girl and I'm sure we'll have fun."

"No we won't," said Henry. "Not with that moody old grouch."

"I'll have fun," said Perfect Peter. "I love having guests."

"She's not sleeping in my room," said Horrid Henry. "She can sleep in the cellar."

"No," said Mom. "You'll move into Peter's room and let Margaret have your bed."

Horrid Henry opened his mouth to scream, but only a rasping sound came out. He was so appalled he could only gasp.

"Give . . . up . . . my . . . room!" he choked. **"To . . . Margaret?"**

Margaret spying on *his* treasures, sleeping in

his bed, playing with *his* toys while he had to share a room with Perfect Peter . . .

"No!" howled Henry. He fell on the floor and screamed. "NO!!"

"I don't mind giving up my bed for a guest," said Perfect Peter. "It's the polite thing to do. Guests come first."

Henry stopped howling just long enough to kick Peter.

"Owww!" screamed Peter. He burst into tears. "Mom!"

"Henry!" yelled Mom. "You horrid boy! Say you're sorry to Peter."

"She's not coming!" shrieked Henry. "And that's final."

"Go to your room!" yelled Mom.

Moody Margaret arrived at Henry's house with her parents, four suitcases, seven boxes of toys, two pillows, and a trumpet.

"Margaret won't be any trouble," said her Mom. "She's always polite, eats everything, and never complains. Isn't that right, Precious?"

"Yes," said Moody Margaret.

"Margaret's not fussy," said her dad. "She's good as gold, aren't you, Precious?"

"Yes," said Moody Margaret.

"Have a lovely vacation," said Mom.

"We will," said Margaret's parents.

The door slammed behind them.

Moody Margaret marched into the sitting room and swept a finger across the mantelpiece.

"It's not very clean, is it?" she said. "You'd never find so much dust at my house."

"Oh," said Dad.

"A little dust never hurt anyone," said Mom.

"I'm allergic," said Margaret. "One whiff of dust and I start to . . . sn . . . sn . . . ACHOOO!" she sneezed.

"We'll clean up right away," said Mom.

Dad mopped.

Mom swept.

Peter dusted.

Henry vacuumed.

Margaret directed.

"Henry, you've missed a big dust-ball right there," said Margaret, pointing under the sofa.

Horrid Henry hovered as far away from the dust as possible.

"Not there, here!" said Margaret.

Henry aimed the vacuum cleaner at Margaret. He was a fire-breathing dragon burning his prey to a crisp.

"Help!" shrieked Margaret.

"Henry!" said Dad.

"Don't be horrid," said Mom.

"I think Henry should be punished," said Moody Margaret. "I think he should be locked in his bedroom for three weeks."

"I don't have a bedroom to be locked up in 'cause you're in it," said Henry. He glared at Margaret.

Margaret glared back.

"I'm the guest, Henry, so you'd better be polite," hissed Margaret.

"Of course he'll be polite," said Mom. "Don't worry, Margaret. Any trouble, you come straight to me."

"Thank you," said Moody Margaret, smiling. "I will. I'm hungry," she added. "Why isn't supper ready?"

"It will be soon," said Dad.

"But I *always* eat at six o'clock," said Margaret. **"I want to eat NOW."**

"All right," said Dad.

Horrid Henry and Moody Margaret dashed for the seat facing the yard. Margaret got there first. Henry shoved her off. Then Margaret shoved him off.

Thud. Henry landed on the floor.

"Ouch," said Henry.

"Let the guest have the chair," said Dad.

"But that's *my* chair," said Henry. "That's where I *always* sit."

"Have my chair, Margaret," said Perfect Peter. "I don't mind."

"I want to sit here," said Moody Margaret. **"I'm the guest, so I decide."**

Horrid Henry dragged himself around the table and sat next to Peter.

"OUCH!" shrieked Margaret. "Henry kicked me!"

"No I didn't," said Henry, outraged.

"Stop it, Henry," said Mom. "That's no way to treat a guest."

Henry stuck out his tongue at Margaret. Moody Margaret stuck out her tongue even further, then stomped on his foot.

"OUCH!" shrieked Henry. "Margaret kicked me!"

Moody Margaret gasped. "Oh, I'm ever so

sorry, Henry," she said sweetly. "It was an accident. Silly me. I didn't mean to, really I didn't."

Dad brought the food to the table.

"What's *that*?" asked Margaret.

"Baked beans, corn on the cob, and chicken," said Dad.

"I don't like baked beans," said Margaret. "And I like my corn off the cob."

Mom scraped the corn off the cob.

"No, put the corn on a separate plate!" shrieked Margaret. **"I don't like vegetables touching my meat."**

Dad got out the pirate plate, the duck plate, and the "Happy birthday, Peter" plate.

"I want the pirate plate," said Margaret, snatching it.

"I want the pirate plate," said Henry, snatching it back.

"I don't mind which plate I get," said Perfect Peter. "A plate's a plate."

"No it isn't!" shouted Henry.

"I'm the guest," shouted Margaret. "I get to choose."

"Give her the pirate plate, Henry," said Dad.

"It's not fair," said Henry, glaring at his plate decorated with little ducks.

"She's the guest," said Mom.

"So?" said Henry. Hadn't there been an ancient Greek who stretched all his guests on an iron bed if they were too short or lopped off their heads and feet if they were too long? That guy sure knew how to deal with horrible guests like Moody Margaret.

"Yuck," said Margaret, spitting out a mouthful of chicken. "You've put salt on it!"

"Only a little," said Dad.

"I never eat salt," said Moody Margaret. "It's not good for me. And I always have peas at my house."

"We'll get some tomorrow," said Mom.

Peter lay asleep in the top bunk. Horrid Henry sat listening by the door. He'd scattered crumbs all over Margaret's bed. He couldn't wait to hear her scream.

But there wasn't a sound coming from Henry's room, where Margaret the invader lay. Henry couldn't understand it.

Sadly, he climbed into—oh, the shame of it—the *bottom* bunk. Then he screamed. His bed was filled with jam, crumbs, and something squishy-squashy and horrible.

"Go to sleep, Henry!" shouted Dad.

That Margaret! **He'd booby-trap the room, cut up her doll's clothes, paint her face purple . . .** Henry smiled grimly. Oh yes, he'd fix Moody Margaret.

Mom and Dad sat in the living room watching TV.

Moody Margaret appeared on the stairs.

"I can't sleep with that noise," she said.

Mom and Dad looked at each other.

"We are watching very quietly, dear," said Mom.

"But I can't sleep if there's any noise in the house," said Margaret. "I have very sensitive ears."

Mom turned off the TV and picked up her knitting needles.

Click, click, click.

Margaret reappeared.

"I can't sleep with that clicking noise," she said.

"All right," said Mom. She sighed a little.

"And it's cold in my bedroom," said Moody Margaret.

Mom turned up the heat.

Margaret reappeared.

"Now it's too hot," said Moody Margaret.

Dad turned down the heat.

"My room smells funny," said Margaret.

"My bed is too hard."

"My room is too stuffy."

"My room is too light."

"Good night, Margaret," said Mom.

"How many more days is she staying?" said Dad.

Mom looked at the calendar.

"Only thirteen," said Mom.

Dad hid his face in his hands.

"I don't know if I can live that long," said Dad.

TOOTA TOOT. Mom blasted out of bed.

TOOTA TOOT. Dad blasted out of bed.

TOOTA TOOT. TOOTA TOOT. TOOTA TOOT TOOT TOOT. Horrid Henry and Perfect Peter blasted out of bed.

Margaret marched down the hall, playing her trumpet.

TOOTA TOOT. TOOTA TOOT. TOOTA TOOT TOOT TOOT TOOT.

"Margaret, would you mind playing your trumpet a little later?" said Dad, clutching his ears. "It's six o'clock in the morning."

"That's when I wake up," said Margaret.

"Could you play a little more softly?" said Mom.

"But I have to practice," said Moody Margaret.

The trumpet blared through the house.

TOOT TOOT TOOT.

Horrid Henry turned on his boom box.

BOOM BOOM BOOM.

Margaret played her trumpet louder.

TOOT! TOOT! TOOT!

Henry blasted his boom box as loud as he could.

BOOM! BOOM! BOOM!

"Henry!" shrieked Mom.

"Turn that down!" bellowed Dad.

"Quiet!" screamed Margaret. "I can't practice with all this noise." She put down her trumpet. "And I'm hungry. Where's my breakfast?"

"We have breakfast at eight," said Mom.

"But I want breakfast now," said Margaret.

Mom had had enough.

"No," said Mom firmly. "We eat at eight."

Margaret opened her mouth and screamed. No one could scream as long, or as loud, as Moody Margaret.

Her piercing screams echoed through the house.

"All right," said Mom. She knew when she was beaten. "We'll eat now."

Henry's diary:

Monday I put crumbs in Margaret's bed. She put jam, crumbs, and slugs in mine.

Tuesday Margaret found my secret cookies and chips and ate every single one.

Wednesday I can't play tapes at night because it disturbs grumpy-face Margaret.

Thursday I can't sing because it disturbs frog-face.

Friday I can't breathe because it disturbs misery-guts.

Saturday

I can stand it No Longer

That night, when everyone was asleep, Horrid Henry crept into the living room and picked up the phone.

"I'd like to send a telegram," he whispered.

Bang, bang, bang, bang, bang.

Ding dong! Ding dong! Ding dong!

Henry sat up in bed.

Someone was banging on the front door and ringing the bell.

"Who could that be at this time of night?" yawned Mom.

Dad peeked through the window, then opened the door.

"Where's my baby?" shouted Moody Margaret's mom.

"Where's my baby?" shouted Moody Margaret's dad.

"Upstairs," said Mom. "Where else?"

"What's happened to her?" cried Margaret's Mom.

"We got here as quick as we could!" shrieked Margaret's dad.

Mom and Dad looked at each other. What was going on?

"She's fine," said Mom.

Margaret's mom and dad looked at each other. What was going on?

"But the telegram said it was an emergency and to come at once," said Margaret's Mom.

"We cut short our vacation," said Margaret's dad.

"What telegram?" said Mom.

"What's going on? I can't sleep with all this noise," said Moody Margaret.

Margaret and her parents had gone home.

"What a terrible mix-up," said Mom.

"Such a shame they cut short their vacation," said Dad.

"Still . . ." said Mom. She looked at Dad.

"Hmmm," said Dad.

"You don't think that Henry . . ." said Mom.

"Not even Henry could do something so horrid," said Dad.

Mom frowned.

"Henry!" said Mom.

Henry continued sticking Peter's stamps together.

"Yeah?"

"Do you know anything about a telegram?"

"Me?" said Henry.

"You," said Mom.

"No," said Henry. "It's a mystery."

"That's a lie, Henry," said Perfect Peter.

"Is not," said Henry.

"Is too," said Peter. "I heard you on the phone."

Henry lunged at Peter. He was a mad bull charging the matador.

"YOWWWWW," shrieked Peter.

Henry stopped. He was in for it now. No allowance for a year. No candy for ten years. No TV ever.

Henry squared his shoulders and waited for his punishment.

Dad put his feet up.

"That was a terrible thing to do," said Dad.

Mom turned on the TV.

"Go to your room," she said.

Henry bounced upstairs. *Your room*. Sweeter words were never spoken.

Chapter 4

HORRID HENRY'S HEAD LICE

Scratch. Scratch. Scratch.

Dad scratched his head.

"Stop scratching, please," said Mom. "We're eating dinner."

Mom scratched her head.

"Stop scratching, please," said Dad. "We're eating dinner."

Henry scratched his head.

"Stop scratching, Henry!" said Mom and Dad.

"Uh-oh," said Mom. She put down her fork and frowned at Henry.

"Henry, do you have lice again?"

"Of course not," said Henry.

"Come over to the sink, Henry," said Mom.

"Why?" said Henry.

"I need to check your head."

Henry dragged his feet over to her as slowly as possible. It's not fair, he thought. It wasn't his fault lice loved him. **Henry's head was a gathering place for lice far and wide.** They probably held lice parties there and foreign lice visited him on their holidays.

Mom dragged the lice comb across Henry's head. She made a face and groaned.

"You're crawling with lice, Henry," said Mom.

"Ooh, let's see," said Henry. He always liked counting how many lice he had.

"One, two, three . . . forty-five, forty-six, forty-seven . . ." he counted, dropping them on to a paper towel.

"It's not polite to count lice," said his younger brother, Perfect Peter, wiping his mouth with his spotless napkin, "is it, Mom?"

"It certainly isn't," said Mom.

Dad dragged the lice comb across his head and made a face.

"Ughh," said Dad.

Mom dragged the comb through her hair.

"Bleeeech," said Mom.

She combed Perfect Peter's hair. Then she did it again. And again. And again.

"No lice, Peter," said Mom, smiling. "As usual. Well done, darling. "

Perfect Peter smiled modestly.

"It's because I wash and comb my hair every night," said Peter.

Henry scowled. True, his hair was filthy, but then . . .

"Lice love clean hair," said Henry.

"No they don't," said Peter. "*I've* never ever had lice."

We'll see about that, thought Henry. When no one was looking he picked a few lice off the paper towel. Then he wandered over to Peter and casually fingered a lock of his hair.

LEAP!

Scratch. Scratch.

"Mom!" squealed Peter. "Henry's pulling my hair!"

"Stop it, Henry," said Dad.

"I wasn't pulling his hair," said Henry indignantly. "I just wanted to see how clean it was. And it is so shiny and clean," added Henry sweetly. "I wish my hair was as clean as Peter's."

Peter beamed. It wasn't often that Henry said anything nice to him.

"Right," said Mom grimly, "everyone upstairs. It's shampoo time. "

"NO!" shrieked Horrid Henry. "NO SHAMPOO!"

He hated the stinky smelly horrible shampoo much more than he hated having lice. Only today his teacher, Miss Battle-Axe, had sent home a louse letter.

Naturally, Henry had crumpled up the letter and thrown it away. He was never ever going to have gross lice shampoo on his head again. What rotten luck Mom had spotted him scratching.

"It's the only way to get rid of lice," said Dad.

"But it never works!" screamed Henry. And he ran for the door.

Mom and Dad grabbed him. Then they dragged him kicking and screaming to the bathroom.

"Lice are living creatures," howled Henry. "Why kill them?"

"Because . . ." said Mom.

"Because . . . because . . . they're bloodsucking lice," said Dad.

Bloodsucking. Henry had never thought of that. In the split second that he stood still to consider this interesting information, Mom emptied the bottle of Supersonic Lice-Blasting Shampoo over his hair.

"NO!" screamed Henry. Frantically, he shook his head. There was shampoo on the door. There was shampoo on the floor. There was shampoo all over Mom and Dad. The only place there was no shampoo was on Henry's head.

"Henry! Stop being horrid!" yelled Dad, wiping shampoo off his shirt.

"What a big fuss over nothing," said Peter.

Henry lunged at him. Mom seized Henry by the collar and held him back.

"Now, Peter," said Mom. "That wasn't a kind

thing to say to Henry, was it? Not everyone is as brave as you."

"You're right, Mom," said Perfect Peter. "I was being rude and thoughtless. It won't happen again. I'm so sorry, Henry."

Mom smiled at him. "That was a perfect apology, Peter. As for you, Henry . . ." She sighed. "We'll get more shampoo tomorrow."

Phew, thought Henry, giving his head an extra-good scratch. **Safe for one more day.**

The next morning at school a group of parents

burst into the classroom, waving the lice letter and shouting.

"My Margaret doesn't have lice!" shrieked Moody Margaret's mother. "She never has and she never will. How dare you send home such a letter!"

"My Josh doesn't have lice," shouted his mother. "The idea!"

"My Toby doesn't have lice!" shouted his father. "Some nasty child in this class isn't bug-busting!"

Miss Battle-Axe squared her shoulders.

"Rest assured that the culprit will be found," she said. "I have declared war on lice. "

Scratch. Scratch. Scratch.

Miss Battle-Axe spun around. Her beady eyes swiveled over the class.

"Who's scratching?" she demanded.

Silence.

Henry bent over his worksheet and tried to look studious.

"Henry is," said Moody Margaret.

"Liar!" shouted Horrid Henry. "It was William!"

Weepy William burst into tears.

"No it wasn't," he sobbed.

Miss Battle-Axe glared at the class.

"I'm going to find out once and for all who's got lice," she growled.

"I don't!" shouted Moody Margaret.

"I don't!" shouted Rude Ralph.

"I don't!" shouted Horrid Henry.

"Silence!" ordered Miss Battle-Axe. "Nora, the lice nurse, is coming this morning. **Who's got lice? Who's not bug-busting?** We'll all find out soon."

Uh-oh, thought Henry. Now I'm sunk. There was no escaping Nurse Nora, Bug Explorer, and her ferocious combs. Everyone would know he had the lice. Rude Ralph would never stop teasing him. He'd be shampooed every night. Mom and Dad would find out about all the lice letters he'd thrown away. . . .

He could of course get a stomachache double quick and be sent home. But Nurse Nora had a horrible way of remembering whose head she hadn't checked and then combing it in front of the whole class.

He could run screaming out the door saying he'd caught mad cow disease. But somehow he didn't think Miss Battle-Axe would believe him.

There was no way out. This time he was well and truly stuck.

Unless . . .

Suddenly Henry had a wonderful, spectacular idea. **It was so wicked, and so horrible, that even Horrid Henry hesitated.** But only for a moment. Desperate times call for desperate measures.

Henry leaned over Clever Clare and brushed his head lightly against hers.

LEAP!

Scratch. Scratch.

"Get away from me, Henry," hissed Clare.

"I was just admiring your lovely picture," said Henry.

He got up to sharpen his pencil. On his way to the sharpener he brushed against Greedy Graham.

LEAP!

Scratch. Scratch.

On his way back from the sharpener Henry

stumbled and fell against Anxious Andrew.

LEAP!

Scratch. Scratch.

"Ow!" yelped Andrew.

"Sorry, Andrew," said Henry. "What big clumsy feet I have. Whoops!" he added, tripping over the carpet and banging heads with Weepy William.

LEAP!

Scratch. Scratch.

"*Waaaaaaaaa!*" wailed William.

"Sit down at once, Henry," said Miss Battle-Axe. "William! Stop scratching. Bert! How do you spell cat?"

"I dunno," said Beefy Bert.

Horrid Henry leaned across the table and put his head close to Bert's.

"C-A-T," he whispered helpfully.

LEAP!

Scratch. Scratch.

Then Horrid Henry raised his hand.

"Yes?" said Miss Battle-Axe. "I don't understand these instructions," said Henry sweetly. "Could you help me, please?"

Miss Battle-Axe frowned. **She liked to keep as far away from Henry as possible.** Reluctantly, she came closer and bent over his work. Henry leaned his head near hers.

LEAP!

Scratch. Scratch.

There was a pounding at the door. Then Nurse Nora marched into the classroom, bristling with combs and other instruments of torture.

"Line up, everyone," said Miss Battle-Axe, patting her hair. "The louse nurse is here."

Rats, thought Henry. He'd hardly started. Slowly he stood up.

Everyone pushed and shoved to be first in line. Then a few children remembered what they were lining up for and stampeded toward the back. Horrid Henry saw his chance and took it.

He charged through the squabbling children, brushing against everyone as fast as he could.

LEAP!

Scratch! Scratch!

LEAP!

Scratch! Scratch!

LEAP!

Scratch! Scratch!

"Henry!" shouted Miss Battle-Axe. "Stay in at recess. Now go to the end of the line. The rest of you, stop this nonsense at once!"

Moody Margaret had fought longest and hardest to be first. Proudly she presented her head to Nurse Nora.

"I certainly don't have lice," she said.

Nurse Nora stuck the comb in.

"Lice!" she announced, stuffing a lice note into Margaret's hand.

For once Margaret was too shocked to speak.

"But . . . but . . ." she gasped.

Tee-hee, thought Henry. Now he wouldn't be the only one.

"Next," said Nurse Nora.

She stuck the comb in Rude Ralph's greasy hair.

"Lice!" she announced.

"Lice-face," hissed Horrid Henry, beside himself with glee.

"Lice!" said Nurse Nora, poking her comb into Lazy Linda's mop.

"Lice!" said Nurse Nora, prodding Greedy Graham's frizzy hair.

"Lice, lice, lice, lice, lice!" she continued, pointing at Weepy William, Clever Clare, Sour Susan, Beefy Bert, and Dizzy Dave.

Then Nurse Nora beckoned to Miss Battle-Axe.

"Teachers, too," she ordered.

Miss Battle-Axe's jaw dropped.

"I have been teaching for twenty-five years and I have never had lice," she said. "Don't waste your time checking me."

Nurse Nora ignored her protests and stuck in the comb.

"Hmmn," she said, and whispered in Miss Battle-Axe's ear.

"NO!" howled Miss Battle-Axe. "NOOOO-OOOOOO!" Then she joined the line of weeping, wailing children clutching their lice notes.

At last it was Henry's turn.

Nurse Nora stuck her comb into Henry's tangled hair and dragged it along his scalp. She combed again. And again. And again.

"No lice," said Nurse Nora. "Keep up the good work, young man."

"I sure will!" said Henry.

Horrid Henry skipped home waving his certificate.

"Look, Peter," crowed Henry. "I'm louse-free!"

Perfect Peter burst into tears.

"I'm not," he wailed.

"What bad luck," said Horrid Henry.